Tippy Lemmey

By Patricia C. McKissack

Illustrated by Susan Keeter

Aladdin Paperbacks

New York London Toronto Sydney Singapore

To my grandson James Everett McKissack

First Aladdin Paperbacks edition January 2003

Text copyright © 2003 by Patricia C. McKissack
Illustrations copyright © 2003 by Susan Keeter

ALADDIN PAPERBACKS
An imprint of Simon & Schuster
Children's Publishing Division
1230 Avenue of the Americas
New York, NY 10020

Designed by Lisa Vega
The text of this book was set in Goudy.

Printed in the United States of America
10 9 8 7 6 5 4 3 2 1

Library of Congress Control Number 2002106064

ISBN 0-689-85019-0

Other books by Patricia C. McKissack

Goin' Someplace Special

The Honest-to-Goodness Truth

Let My People Go

Ma Dear's Aprons

NEW DOG IN TOWN

In 1951 there was a war going on in a place called Korea. My friends Paul and Jeannie and I were fighting our own war. In Templeton, Tennessee, where we lived, the enemy was a new dog in town. His name was Tippy Lemmey. He was the only dog I ever knew who had a first and last name.

To get anywhere, we had to use Settler's Pike. But the problem was getting past Tippy Lemmey. When we rode on our bicycles, he chased us. He barked. He growled. He snapped at our heels.

He was a monster—always waiting, ready to attack. When we ran, he came after us. When we crossed the street, he followed. No getting away from him. Over him. Or under him.

He belonged to the Lemmeys. They were an ordinary couple who bought the Wilson place and tried to fix it up. Still it remained as plain as the Lemmeys themselves. There was nothing plain or ordinary about their dog, though.

Tippy Lemmey had reddish fluffy fur and a tongue that looked like he'd been chewing on a sour-grape sucker. He had a curled-up tail and a sweet teddy-bear face. But take it from me—there was nothing kind about that dog. He had the heart of an alligator.

The Lemmeys built a plain, white fence around their plain, white house. They should have known that nothing so ordinary could hold Tippy Lemmey. He leaped over it easily.

If we wanted to win our war, then we needed a plan. . . .

THE PLAN

One of our favorite play spots was Ashland Bridge. It had two levels. One was a road, and the other was a railroad track. The bridge had been used while the mill was open. The mill closed, so the bridge wasn't used anymore. It was all ours to play on.

Paul, Jeannie, and I hadn't been going to our special spot much. Tippy Lemmey stood in our way. We mostly met under the big oak in my backyard.

Behind my house there was a backwater branch,

dry most of the time, until it rained. Then it filled up with fast-moving water.

Mama forbade me to play in the branch—especially if it looked like rain. The oak stood far enough away from the branch that when my friends and I sat under it, I wasn't disobeying.

"Let's rock Tippy Lemmey," said Paul. He picked up a smooth stone and threw it at a stump. Paul was eight. So was Jeannie. I would be eight on August ninth. Paul liked talking tough. But he wasn't mean.

"Two wrongs don't make a right," said Jeannie, peeling an orange. She had just had a big birthday party. She got a new bike.

Jeannie liked grown-up talk. She repeated things her grandmother said. Paul and I were never sure what the sayings meant. Truth is, Jeannie didn't know either. But this time we agreed that throwing rocks at the dog wouldn't make matters any better.

We talked about one thing and then another. Then suddenly Jeannie had an idea. Passing out orange wedges to each one of us, she explained. "We're smarter than a dog. Let's just trick him." She laid out her plan. It sounded reasonable. She was so sure of her plan; Paul and I believed it might work, too. Almost.

So we pulled straws. I lost. According to the plan, I had to ride front and center. Paul and Jeannie rode behind me and on either side.

Tippy Lemmey was waiting as usual. When Jeannie saw him she shouted, "Go! Go! Go for your life!"

Just as we planned, I pumped hard and pushed straight down the middle. Paul and Jeannie took turns crossing over from side to side. They moved in and out. To let Jeannie tell it, that was supposed to confuse Tippy Lemmey. It didn't.

At first he stopped running. He stood there on short, stocky legs. His beady eyes looked like black pools of tar. Then lowering his head he took off after me like a fireball—snarling and growling, snipping and snapping at my heels.

When I looked around, my friends had left me

behind. I was screaming and yelling, riding with my legs up on the handlebars. I managed to escape, but I was out of breath. My legs felt like rubber bands.

"Well, Jeannie, so much for your bright ideas. It seems the dog is smarter than you," I said, gulping in air. I tried not to cry.

Paul buried his face in the soft green grass. "Tippy Lemmey is no ordinary dog," he said.

Jeannie's eyes were as large as half-dollars. "Unbelievable! He thinks like people."

FROM BAD TO WORSE

Being chased by Tippy Lemmey going to and from school was bad enough. At least I had my buddies. But come Saturdays I had to face him alone.

My piano lessons were at 9:30 sharp. To get to Miss Dickerson's house, I first had to get by Tippy Lemmey.

One morning Tippy was chasing me, and I lost my balance. *Wham!* I hit the ground. The wind blew my sheet music all around like giant snowflakes. Fortunately Tippy Lemmey started growling and jumping at the paper. That gave me just enough time to grab a few pieces and escape. My heart was still pounding when I reached Miss Dickerson's house with ripped music.

That horrible dog didn't even take a rest on Sundays. He made us run and sweat in our good clothes.

"We've got to do something," said Paul after we'd been chased one Sunday morning. He wiped his face with the back of his hand. His white shirt was wrinkled. His blue pants were dirty. His best shoes were scuffed. He had kicked up a lot of dust, running from Tippy Lemmey.

Jeannie and I didn't look any better. In the chase Jeannie had torn the hem of her dress. I had lost my good ribbons, and my thick braids were coming undone. My hair was all over my head. I looked like a wild woman.

We couldn't go to Sunday school like that. So instead we went over to our special spot at Ashland

Bridge. We were losing the war—badly. We needed another plan of attack.

"What if we tell on him?" said Jeannie.

"Tell who?" I asked.

"I'm going to put my daddy on him," she said, hands on her hips. "Like my grandma always says, 'There's more than one way to skin a cat.'"

"What does a cat have to do with a dog?" Paul asked. He took off his shoes and swung his legs over the side of the bridge.

Jeannie tried to make sense of what she'd said. "My daddy can fix anything—dog, cat, rat—makes no difference. He caught a big ol' snake that was living in our garage and . . ."

"Okay we get the point," Paul said.

I took off my best shoes and white lace socks. The sun felt warm on my legs. I wiggled my toes and giggled. It felt so good. For a moment I didn't care about Tippy Lemmey. I didn't worry about losing the handkerchief Granny Bea had sent me for

Christmas. Last I saw of it, Tippy was eating it.

"What do you think, Leandra? Should we tell our folks?" Paul asked me.

"We can. But all they'll say is, 'It's just a little dog. There's nothing to be frightened of,'" I answered.

Paul nodded. "My mother insists that there's no such thing as monsters."

"And we all know better," I added.

"This is different," Jeannie put in. "Tippy Lemmey is a living, breathing monster—with a first and last name. They can see him. Hear him. They will have to do something."

There we sat, side by side, with our legs dangling over the side of the bridge, hoping that our parents would join the war as our allies.

"Okay. We'll tell," I said.

"Last one to the Pike is a dead fly," said Paul, leaping to his feet. In a flash, he hopped onto his bike and was off. Jeannie and I followed right on his heels.

YOU'RE GOING TO GET IT, TIPPY LEMMEY

I was so scared of Tippy Lemmey and just as tired of running. It felt good to tell Mama and Daddy about him.

"Tippy Lemmey has made my life miserable," I said. I struggled hard to hold back the tears. "He's mean. He chases Jeannie and Paul, too. I'm afraid he's going to get me."

Mama held me close. Daddy sat beside us on the bed. "How long has this been going on?" he asked.

"Since Mr. and Mrs. Lemmey moved here," I answered.

Daddy gave Mama a questioning look. Mama explained. "They are an elderly couple. They bought the Wilson place out on the Pike. We don't know much about them." Daddy nodded.

"I'm so scared of Tippy Lemmey," I said. I couldn't stop the tears from coming. "He's a real monster."

"Oh, sweet pea." Daddy hugged me up close. "Don't you worry. I'll handle this! You did right, coming to us about it."

That night, I felt like *my* daddy could make the world right again. "Look out, Tippy Lemmey," I whispered. "You're going to get it."

Morning came. Daddy took off from work at the garage. He and Mama walked with me to the Lemmeys' house. To my surprise, neither Jeannie nor Paul was anywhere to be seen. Tippy Lemmey either.

Daddy rang the doorbell. I hung back, not knowing what to expect. "Be careful."

Mr. Lemmey answered the door. "Hello. May I help you?" he asked. I'd only seen Mr. Lemmey from a distance. I really didn't know what to expect. He had on a plain white shirt and dark blue pants. But he had a very pleasant smile and the happiest eyes I'd ever seen.

"My name is Harvey Martin," Daddy said, extending his hand. "This is my wife, Pearlie, and my daughter, Leandra. The only child I have. And I love her as much as heaven will allow."

Mr. Lemmey shook Daddy's hand, up and down like a seesaw. "I know that proud feeling. I have a son whom I love just that much too."

THE LION'S DEN

Realizing that we were standing in the doorway, Mr. Lemmey invited us in. I looked past him into the monster's den. Wonder of wonders. It was neat and orderly. No bones lying around. Nothing special at all.

"Do come in," Mr. Lemmey insisted.

What a nice man, I thought. *How could he own such a mean dog?* Mr. Lemmey smiled at me warmly. I looked away. There was no way I was going into the lion's den. I took Daddy's hand and pulled back.

Daddy stood still. "No, Mr. Lemmey," he said. "I thank you for the offer. But not this time. You see, I've come here about your son, I think."

Suddenly Mr. Lemmey's face went pale. Worry filled his eyes. My face must have changed too. Son? What was Daddy talking about? Then it hit me like a piece of falling sky. Daddy thought Tippy Lemmey was a boy.

I was amazed at how things can get so twisted.

Mr. Lemmey gasped. "My son?" He closed the door and stepped out on the porch. He whispered. "What? What has happened? Tell me what you know before my wife comes."

I wanted the earth to open up and swallow me in one big bite.

"Well," said Daddy, who suspected nothing, "your son, Tippy Lemmey, has been giving my daughter a very hard time."

"No, Daddy," I tried to whisper. "You got it all wrong."

But before I could finish, Mama shushed me and jumped right in, saying, "Your son has been bullying our daughter. He's made Leandra's life miserable. She's afraid to go to school, to music lessons, to church, anywhere."

"No, Mama, it's not . . ." I tried really hard to get their attention. But . . .

"Don't be scared," Daddy said, taking my arm. "See how terrified she is? Your son's been chasing her almost every day."

Mr. Lemmey looked confused, then slowly a big smile broke across his face. I knew why. When Mama and Daddy finished, all Mr. Lemmey could do was laugh.

He started laughing and couldn't stop. Taking a seat in one of the porch chairs, he sighed deeply. "Please forgive me," he said. "I'm laughing because I'm relieved that you aren't talking about my son, Curtis Lemmey. He's a soldier in Korea. I thought for a moment something might have happened to him.

Tippy Lemmey is my son's *dog*. We are keeping him until Curtis returns."

Mama flashed a half-smile. "Oh," she said. She looked straight at me. I dropped my head.

"Tippy Lemmey is a—a—a dog? Whoever heard of a dog with a first and last name?" Daddy put in.

"My son's idea," Mr. Lemmey answered, still laughing.

Daddy tried to save face. He pulled himself tall. "The way Leandra tells it, your dog—or your son's dog—is pretty vicious. He's terrorized all the kids in the neighborhood." Daddy wasn't giving up.

"What's going on out here?" said Mrs. Lemmey coming to the door. She was a small woman with a halo of white hair. "Oh! Guests." She clapped her hands. "And look at me. I've been giving the puppy a bath. Been drying him on the back porch."

The puppy? *Could she possibly be talking about Tippy Lemmey?*

MONSTERS ARE
LIKE THAT

Mrs. Lemmey offered Mama a seat. "Won't you please have a cold drink? Cup of coffee, maybe?"

"They're here about Tippy," said Mr. Lemmey. "They say he's terrorizing the neighborhood children."

"Oh, my. Has Tippy been bad?" said Mrs. Lemmey. "He's such a sweet puppy."

Puppy? Sweet?

Mr. Lemmey whistled. Tippy came running to the door. I grabbed Daddy's hand. *Now they'd find out the truth*, I thought.

Mrs. Lemmey opened the door for Tippy to come out. Mama choked back a scream. I jumped behind Daddy. And he braced himself for a possible attack. Tippy rushed out the door, barking, jumping and leaping like a mad squirrel.

"No need to be afraid. Sit," said Mrs. Lemmey gently. "Sit, boy." The dog obeyed. He sat as still as he could. But his tail twitched from side to side. "Good puppy."

I wanted to say, "There's nothing good about him."

"Come, Tippy. Salute Mr. and Mrs. Martin," said Mr. Lemmey. "Our son Curtis taught him this before leaving for Korea."

Tippy sat up on his hind legs and placed his paw by the side of his head.

"Ahhh." Mama sighed, as if cooing at a baby.

She was being suckered in. Couldn't she see that this was all just an act?

For ten minutes or more, Tippy Lemmey rolled

over and shook hands with Daddy. He licked Mama's hand too.

"He's big, but still just a puppy. He loves to play," said Mrs. Lemmey. "Come," she said calling me. "Make friends with him, dear. He won't bite."

"Only because you're here," I said, stepping back. "Monsters are like that. They fool adults into believing they're harmless. But we kids know a monster when we see one. Tippy Lemmey is not a good dog. He chases us on our bicycles. He snarls and snaps at our heels. He's a for-real monster."

Mrs. Lemmey looked sad. "Oh, honey, Tippy isn't chasing you. He gets excited about the turning wheels. It's a game—a time to play with you children. He wouldn't harm a thing."

Mr. and Mrs. Lemmey offered to keep Tippy tied up so we could pass to and from school without being chased. When school was out for summer, though, Tippy could run free again. Mama and Daddy were convinced that Tippy was no threat to me. So they agreed.

"He's not vicious at all," said Mama.

"He's playful," said Daddy. Then they both recited the parents' theme: "You're a big girl now. There's nothing to be afraid of."

NOW WHAT?

I couldn't wait to tell my friends everything that had happened. "You should have seen Tippy Lemmey acting like a puppy," I said, feeling real disgusted.

"If Tippy is a puppy, then what will he be like when he grows up?" Jeannie asked.

"A bigger, meaner dog than any of us has ever seen," answered Paul.

Early the next morning we rode slowly past Tippy Lemmey's house. As usual, he was on the front porch . . . waiting. When he saw us he dashed toward the fence. We were ready to take off. But suddenly the rope jerked. Tippy Lemmey was stopped in his tracks.

We sent up a loud cheer! The monster had been tied up. We rode around in circles right under his nose. We knew he couldn't get to us.

For two wonderful days we rode to and from school in peace. On the third morning, Paul decided to tease Tippy. "*Try, try, hard as you can,*" Paul chanted. "*You can't catch me, I'm the gingerbread man!*"

We took up the song. "*Try, try, hard as you can. You can't catch him, he's the gingerbread man.*" We rode around and around, making big figure eights.

All Tippy Lemmey could do was watch.

We sang louder as we rode in wider circles, faster and faster. "*Try, try, hard as you can. . . .*"

Suddenly Tippy Lemmey let out something that sounded like a roar. He bounded off the porch and headed straight for us. We weren't worried. The rope was sure to stop him.

But it didn't.

The rope snapped in two. Tippy Lemmey kept coming—barking, snarling, and growling. He leaped over the fence. And before we knew what was happening, he was upon us.

We rode like the wind. But Tippy Lemmey was faster.

"The cat's out of the bag," said Jeannie, throwing her arms in the air.

Paul and I said at the same time: "Girl! Tippy Lemmey is not a cat!"

The monster was loose again. Now what?

AN ESCAPE ROUTE

Mr. Lemmey explained that Tippy had chewed through the rope. "It won't happen again. I'm using a chain this time. It will hold him."

We weren't as sure. "Tippy can probably chew through a chain," said Paul.

So we rode by each morning quickly. And we dared Paul to sing.

When school ended a few weeks later, Tippy Lemmey was free again.

"If he chases you," said Mr. Lemmey, "don't run.

Stop. Then say in a stern way, 'No, Tippy Lemmey. No. Go home!' See what happens."

Jeannie was sure Mr. Lemmey was just kidding us. "He can't think we'd really do that?"

Mrs. Lemmey tried too. She invited Jeannie and me to stop by anytime. "It gets lonely out here. All our friends are back in Ohio. So come by. Get to know Tippy better," she said. "He really is a dear."

She seemed sad when we said no—even though we were careful to be polite.

Jeannie and I were out by the big oak talking about our problem. With Tippy running free, we were grounded. No way to get to the Ashland Bridge. Suddenly we heard Paul calling us from behind.

"Over here," Paul shouted. He was coming out of the dry branch. He was excited about something. "I've found a way to get around Tippy Lemmey." He waved for us to come with him. "All we have to do is follow the dry branch. It goes under the Pike and comes out at the old abandoned mill. Beyond there is

Ashland Creek, and downstream is our bridge."

"It's a clear route around Tippy Lemmey," Jeannie shouted. She hopped on her bicycle. But I didn't follow right away.

Mama forbade me to play in the branch. But the sky was clear—not a wisp of a cloud. And besides, I told myself, I wasn't going to *play* in the branch. It was nothing more than an escape route.

"Let's go!" I shouted.

GONE FOREVER

From then on we used the escape route to get to Ashland Bridge. We hadn't seen Tippy Lemmey in days. I was uneasy about disobeying Mama. I always watched the sky, though. If it looked cloudy, I found a reason to stay home.

One morning the three of us decided to go swimming at Settler's Beach at the lake. It was at least a two-mile ride. We followed the dry branch to where it went under the Pike. Once there, we heard dogs barking.

Fearful that Tippy Lemmey was nearby, we stopped. We stayed very quiet and listened.

"I found this one running along the road," a man said, getting out of a faded blue truck.

We eased up the bank so we could see and hear better. To our surprise a tall, thin man with bushy eyebrows stood beside the truck. Right next to him was Tippy Lemmey.

He had captured our enemy in a net. Tippy struggled to get free, but the harder he pulled, the more tangled he became. He was trapped.

But what were those men planning to do with him? I wondered. We could hear more dogs barking in the abandoned mill house.

"This one is a chow," said another man, coming into view. He was younger than the first man by twenty years or more. He had an eagle tattooed on his forearm.

"That makes six dogs now," the young man said. "All full-bred: a collie, a bulldog, a beagle, two hunting hounds, and this chow."

"On the other side of the state we can sell these dogs for lots of money," the older man said. "Let's plan to leave here as soon as it gets dark."

The two thieves closed the tailgate. Then we watched as they carried Tippy Lemmey into the mill and shut the door.

We said nothing until we reached Ashland Bridge. Then we cheered and laughed for joy.

"Good-bye, Tippy Lemmey. We won't miss you," said Paul.

"That ol' dog is getting what he deserves," said Jeannie.

We cheered and clapped and kicked up our heels. Then we stopped cheering and sat quietly. I was thinking about poor Mr. and Mrs. Lemmey. What would they tell their son when he came home from Korea? He was fighting for our country, in a war far, far away, and it didn't seem right that we just let his dog get stolen by two creeps. I wondered what Paul and Jeannie were thinking.

HAVE A HEART

"I'm going home," I said. Jeannie agreed.

Paul shrugged. "Me too."

Paul reminded us that we didn't have to use the escape route. On the way home we didn't talk much.

Just as we were about to go by the Lemmey house, Mr. Lemmey came charging out.

"Children!" he shouted. "Wait one moment."

We stopped. He was breathless. "Have you seen Tippy anywhere? He's been gone all morning. He

doesn't answer my call. That's very unusual. I do hope he hasn't run off."

"He hasn't run away," I said, being very careful not to lie. But I wasn't being truthful, either. "I've got to go," I said. "Got to get home in time for lunch."

I rode away fast. Paul and Jeannie followed.

"If you see him, please let me know," Mr. Lemmey called after us. "Mrs. Lemmey is beginning to worry."

Back under the big oak tree, we shared peanut butter-and-jelly sandwiches Mama made.

"I should be glad Tippy Lemmey is going . . . going . . . gone! Good riddance," said Jeannie. "But I'm not glad."

I felt relieved that I wasn't the only one having those kinds of feelings. "I don't like Tippy Lemmey either," I said. "But I don't like the idea that he's been stolen. Those thieves don't have a right to do that."

Paul finished the last of his milk. "I think the thieves have done us a great favor. They got rid of our bitter enemy," he answered.

"Oh, come on, Paul," said Jeannie. "Have a heart."

"Think about the Lemmeys," I said. "They are such nice people who have tried to help us."

Jeannie turned away from Paul. "Leandra," she said to me, "What should we do?"

"I think we should try to help all those poor dogs," I said. "Including Tippy Lemmey."

"Traitor," Paul scoffed. "You're aiding the enemy."

"I've made up my mind." I hopped on my bike and started down the dry branch. "Who's with me?"

Far in the distance, I thought I heard thunder.

SEARCH AND RESCUE

Jeannie caught up with me. I knew she would.

The dog thieves said they were going to leave at sunset. It was daylight until almost eight o'clock. We had time, but we moved fast.

When we reached the old mill house, the faded blue truck was gone. We circled around and came up on the backside of the old shack.

"Hey!" It was Paul, catching up from behind. Jeannie and I both jumped in fear.

"Don't sneak up on us like that," I said, giving him a shove.

"Thought you didn't want to aid the enemy." Jeannie got in a word jab.

Paul's whole face grinned. "This is better than a movie. I didn't want to miss it. You might need me anyhow."

He was right. I stood on his shoulders to get a look in one of the dirty windows. The two thieves were gone. All the dogs they had captured were tied up inside.

We hurried around to the front door. It had a big padlock on it. I felt the first raindrop.

Thinking quickly, Paul found a loose board and pulled it back. It was just enough space for me to crawl through. Once inside I began untying the dogs.

They ran to the hole. One by one they escaped.

"Come on, it's raining pretty hard," Paul called to me.

Tippy Lemmey was the last dog I untied. When he was free, he leaped into my arms, knocking me down.

"So this is the thanks I get for saving you?!" I shouted. Then I realized that Tippy Lemmey was trembling . . . trembling from fear. Without thinking, I let my hand pet his head. "It's okay. You're okay now," I whispered. Tippy Lemmey started licking my hands and face. Yuck!

"Hurry," said Jeannie who was the lookout. "I think I hear them coming over the old bridge."

I shoved Tippy through the hole. "Run!" I yelled. And Tippy took off like a missile. While he was climbing out, the faded blue truck came clambering up the road.

It was raining hard.

"What?!" the younger thief shouted. "What are you kids doing?" The older man leaped out and rushed toward us.

All the dogs were free. But we weren't. With the roadway blocked, the only way to run was into the dry branch. We didn't even have time to pick up our bikes. And it was pouring.

HELP

The dognappers chased us a little ways. But one of them slipped and fell. It was raining so hard, they decided to stop.

"Ah, let 'em go," said the older thief. He waved his hands. "Let's get out of here. There are always plenty of dogs in other places."

At least they weren't chasing us anymore. But we had another problem. The branch was quickly filling with water. It was getting harder and harder to run. Jeannie kept falling.

We heard a roaring sound. When we looked behind us, a flash of water was coming. We tried to climb out, but the banks were too slippery and the water was coming too fast.

In the nick of time, Paul reached for a low-hanging tree limb with one hand. He grabbed my hand with the other. I took Jeannie's hand in mine and held on for dear life. The water crashed into us. It flipped and flopped us around like clothes on a line. But none of us let go.

Suddenly we saw Tippy Lemmey on the opposite bank. He ran back and forth, barking and barking.

"Go, Tippy. Go get help!" I shouted. "Now!" Tippy ran away barking like a hound after a rabbit.

"You don't honestly think that dog is going to go get help, do you?" Paul scoffed. "He's not Lassie."

"I know, but maybe . . . ," I said, spitting water out of my mouth.

Paul tried to pull up on the branch. He couldn't. The limb cracked a little.

"Hold still!" Jeannie shouted. "Don't move."

"My arms feel like they're coming off," Paul said.

My arm hurt too. I couldn't let Jeannie go. But I felt her hand slipping out of mine.

"I—I—I can't hold on to you anymore!" Paul cried out. And he let go of my hand. At the same time I let go of Jeannie. All three of us fell into the dark, muddy water. We kicked and splashed and kicked. When we calmed down and stood up, the water only came to our shoulders. It had stopped raining. We weren't going to drown after all.

Not far off we heard the familiar bark of Tippy Lemmey. And Mr. Lemmey calling us. Tippy *was* bringing help.

THE GREATEST

"Tippy told me something was wrong," said Mr. Lemmey. "He barked and barked until I followed him here." He pulled Jeannie out of the branch. She was covered in mud from head to foot. "I came as soon as I figured out what he was saying."

"Golly, Molly," said Paul. "Tippy Lemmey did bring help—just like Lassie."

Mr. Lemmey hurried us to his house. Mrs. Lemmey turned the garden hose on us, and we had a good time cleaning up until the police came. We told them the whole story. I described the thieves. Jeannie described the truck. She was so dramatic. Paul impressed everyone when he remembered the license plate number. It was just like in the movies.

All the while Tippy Lemmey sat beside me. I reached down and rubbed behind his ears. Mrs. Lemmey saw me and smiled. "See, I knew you two would be friends," she said.

"If your enemy saves your life, does that still make him your enemy?" Jeannie asked.

Mr. Lemmey chuckled. "I think you've found out something about Tippy Lemmey: He really isn't all that bad."

"In my book, he's the greatest," I said.

To the Lemmeys we were heroes. But not in Mama's eyes. When she heard about us being in the dry creek bed, I got a weeklong punishment. She called Jeannie and Paul's parents, too. They got the same. And they blamed me.

Five full days passed. Pure torture. "Freedom!"

Paul shouted on the first day we could ride again.

It felt wonderful to have my wheels back. First thing, we headed for Ashland Bridge. Tippy Lemmey was waiting for us. He came charging over the fence barking, snarling, and growling. He was back to his old self again.

Paul and Jeannie rode ahead of me. But I threw on the brakes. "Stop!" I shouted. I held out my arm. Tippy Lemmey stopped. "Go back. Go back!"

Tippy Lemmey lowered his head and turned away. He looked wounded. Suddenly I realized that Mrs. Lemmey was right. Tippy Lemmey was just a big puppy.

"Okay. Come on," I said. "Come."

Like a flash, Tippy Lemmey was all over me jumping, turning, and licking my hands.

PEACE

I've never known another animal like Tippy Lemmey. He was the only dog I ever met who had a first and last name.

During the rest of that memorable summer of 1951, Tippy Lemmey waited for us to ride by his house. He'd dash off the porch and leap over the fence. But he didn't run after us. He ran with us.

Tippy was our constant companion. He loved romping through the woods and fields with Paul. They'd wrestle for hours on a carpet of grass. And splash in the cool water of Ashland Creek.

Other times Tippy allowed Jeannie to squeeze him like a real live teddy bear. And play hospital with her new doctor's kit. "Tippy Lemmey is such a good patient," she'd say.

But when Tippy's patience ran out, or when he was tired of running or wrestling, he'd come and flop near me. And I'd rub his head.

Mrs. Lemmey was beside herself with joy. "All of you are just getting along so nicely," she said. She fixed us cookies by the dozens and lemonade by the gallons. Mr. Lemmey read poems to us from books. Several of them he had written himself.

Whenever they received a letter from their son, Curtis, the Lemmeys shared it with us. One time he thanked us for being friends with his dog. That made us smile.

On my eighth birthday, Mrs. Lemmey gave me a pocket handkerchief. It was almost just like the one Tippy had ripped apart. She had crocheted a lovely *L* for "Leandra" on it. Many years later, I still have it.

We all hoped the war in Korea would end soon, and the boys would come home. But as for Paul, Jeannie, and me, our war was over.